THE SPINNER'S GIFT

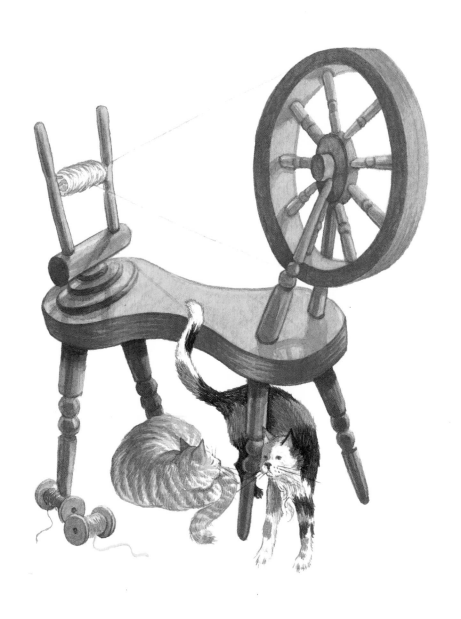

The Spinner's Gift

A TALE BY **Gail Radley**

ILLUSTRATED BY

Paige Miglio

North-South Books

NEW YORK ❧ LONDON

ONCE A QUEEN was preparing for a great ball to which kings and queens of nearby lands would be invited. She called for her seamstress and said, "I must have a new gown unlike any in this land or the next."

"For this I must have the finest cloth," said the seamstress, so she went to tell the weaver.

"For this I must have the finest thread," said the weaver, so he went to tell the spinner.

Now the spinner was a poor woman who lived at the edge of the village. Though most often she was called upon to spin for coarse ropes and fishing nets, the weaver knew she could spin a fine thread, and this he asked her to do.

The spinner worked at the wheel for six days. She spun several hanks of fine thread, which she carefully bleached and dyed. Some of it was as white as new fallen snow, some as gold as the blazing midday sun and some as red as the roses in the queen's own garden. When she was finished she put the thread on wooden reels and delivered them to the weaver.

The weaver held up the thread. It seemed to shine in the sunlight. "This thread is unlike any in this land or the next," he told her. "You have done well."

The weaver worked at his loom for three days, blending the threads into a lovely, delicate pattern, then he delivered the cloth to the royal seamstress.

The seamstress looked at the cloth. "Ah!" she cried. "It's lovely, the pattern so delicate. You have done well."

The seamstress cut and sewed the cloth into a new gown unlike any in this land or the next.

The queen was well-pleased and wore the gown at the ball where everyone marveled at its beauty.

Time passed and the queen had a daughter who loved beautiful things. The princess especially loved her mother's gown, and because the queen loved her so, she had the dress cut down and altered and gave it to her daughter on her thirteenth birthday.

But soon the young princess had outgrown the gown and passed it along to one of her maids who had admired it.

The maid wore it only twice, for she realized it was too fine a gown to wear at the palace. It was lovelier than even those worn by the queen or the princess and she was but a maid. But rather than put it away where no one could enjoy it, she gave it to the jeweler's wife.

By this time, the dress was beginning to look a bit shabby. "It was a fine dress in its time," the jeweler's wife said, "but I've nowhere to wear such a gown anyway. It will make handsome curtains." And she cut it down for curtains and hung them in her sitting room.

Some months later, a thief slipped into the jeweler's house by night. As he was filling his sack with jewels, he saw the handsome curtains. "Such beautiful cloth," he said to himself. "Those curtains will bring a good price somewhere." So he stuffed them into his sack with the jewels.

But the thief didn't have time to tie up his sack for the jeweler and his wife had heard him and came running out. The thief leapt through the window and made for the forest. Along the way, one curtain fell out of his sack.

A dog found the curtain in the field, carried it off in his teeth to the edge of the forest, and slept on it.

The next day a peddler happened to pass that way and saw the dirty cloth wadded up on the ground. He picked it up and looked at it closely.

"This was once a lovely bit of cloth," he said to himself, and washed it in the stream and put it in his pack.

That evening, he came by the poor spinner's house.

"Good woman," said he. "I've not had a real meal in a fortnight. Could you offer a poor peddler some food?"

The spinner shared her soup and bread with him and gave him cheese for his journey.

"Let me repay your kindness," said the peddler. "Please take something from my pack—anything you like."

What the spinner loved best was the piece of cloth. It was ragged now and had darkened with age. The white looked like fresh cream, the gold was as deep as the setting sun and the red was as dark as clustered grapes on the arbor. But still it delighted her and she took it, not knowing it came from the thread she herself had spun and dyed years before.

By this time the old queen had passed away. The princess had married a prince from a nearby land and was soon to have a child.

When the baby was born, everyone in the kingdom brought the baby a gift, for the princess was well-loved.

"I have made her a silver spoon," said the silversmith. "See how it shines."
"I have made her a tall candle of my clearest wax," said the candlemaker.

"Oh, dear," said the spinner, when the candlemaker gave her the news. "I have nothing fit for the princess's baby, and there is not time to spin thread for her clothing." She looked about her house until she saw the piece of cloth. Only a small square of it was not ragged and she cut this out and took it to the princess.

"It is only a scrap of cloth," said the spinner, looking down at her feet, "but it is the nicest thing I have."

The princess held the scrap up to the sunlight. "Why it reminds me of a gown I once had—it was cut down from my mother's dress. It was as white as the newly fallen snow, as gold as the blazing midday sun, and as red as the roses in my mother's own garden."

The spinner looked up and saw that the princess was smiling.

"The pattern was lovely, like this, and it was made of the finest cloth, woven from the finest thread," the princess went on. "Thank you, good woman."

From the scrap the princess made a quilt to cover the baby's bed—and a well-loved quilt it was.

JE

With love to Jana, who has had many hand-me-downs. –G.R.
To my Mother and Father, for all their love, support, and patience. –P.M.

Text copyright © 1994 by Gail Radley
Illustrations copyright © 1994 by Paige Miglio

Published in the United States by North-South Books Inc., New York.

Published simultaneously in Great Britain, Canada, Australia, and
New Zealand in 1994 by North-South Books, an imprint of
Nord-Süd Verlag AG, Gossau Zürich, Switzerland.

Library of Congress Cataloging-in-Publication Data is available.
A CIP catalogue record for this book is available from The British Library.
ISBN 1-55858-325-4 (TRADE EDITION)
ISBN 1-55858-326-2 (LIBRARY EDITION)

Typography by Marc Cheshire
1 3 5 7 9 TB 10 8 6 4 2
1 3 5 7 9 LB 10 8 6 4 2
Printed in Belgium